Suddenly!

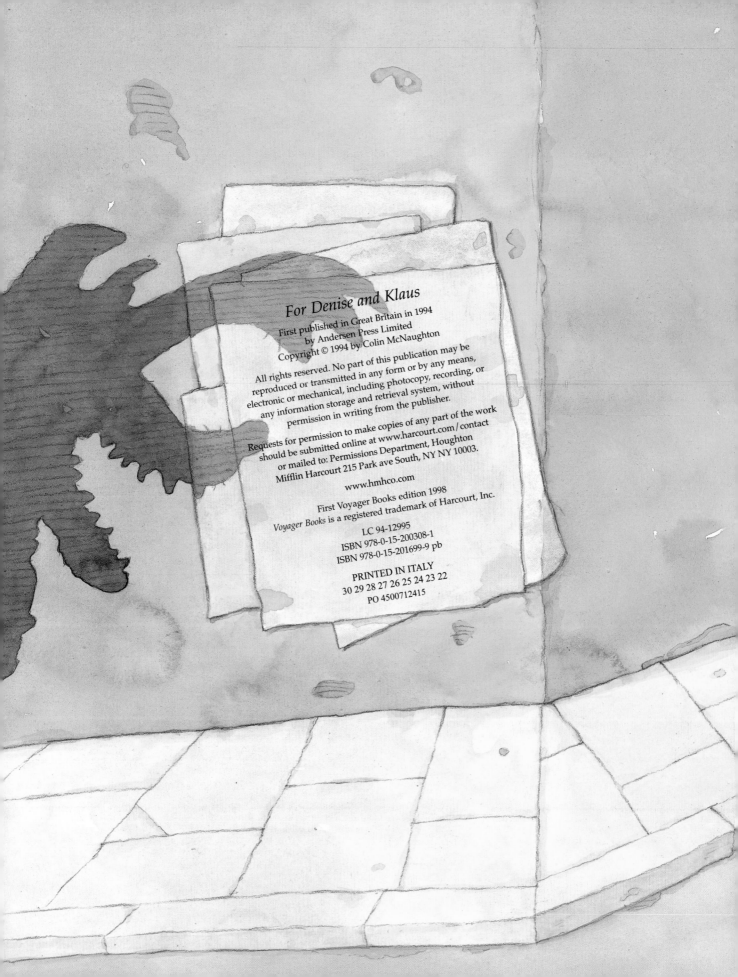

For Denise and Klaus

First published in Great Britain in 1994
by Andersen Press Limited
Copyright © 1994 by Colin McNaughton

www.hmhco.com

First Voyager Books edition 1998
Voyager Books is a registered trademark of Harcourt, Inc.

LC 94-12995
ISBN 978-0-15-200308-1
ISBN 978-0-15-201699-9 pb

PRINTED IN ITALY
30 29 28 27 26 25 24 23 22
PO 4500712415

Suddenly!

WORDS AND PICTURES BY

Colin McNaughton

Voyager Books
Harcourt, Inc.

ORLANDO AUSTIN NEW YORK SAN DIEGO TORONTO LONDON

Preston was walking home
from school one day when
suddenly!

Preston remembered
his mother had asked
him to go to the store.

Preston was doing
the shopping when

suddenly!

He dashed out of the
store! He remembered
he had left the grocery
money in his school desk.

Preston got the money
from his desk and
was coming out of
the school when

suddenly!

Preston decided to use
the back door.

On his way back to the store
Preston stopped by the park
to play when

suddenly!

Billy the bully
shoved past him and
went down the slide!

Preston climbed down
from the slide and went
on to do the shopping.
He was just coming out
of the store when

suddenly!

Mr. Plimp the storekeeper called Preston back to say he had forgotten his change.

At last Preston arrived
home. " Mom," he said,
"I've had the strangest
feeling that someone
has been following me."
Suddenly!

Preston's mother turned around and gave him an enormous

hug!

nee-naa-nee-naa-nee-naa-nee-n

WOLF HOSPITAL →